Just then, she heard somebody outside her mousehole.

That's right, Little Miss Tiny is so tiny she lives in a mousehole, in the skirting board, in the dining room, in Home Farm.

It was Mr Daydream. "I was on my way to see Father Christmas," he said. "Would you like to come along on a Christmas holiday with me?"

Little Miss Tiny could not believe her luck.

If it really was luck.

Waiting outside was Mr Daydream's magic bird.

Mr Daydream's enormous, yellow, magic bird.

Enormous to you or I, but as big as the moon to Little Miss Tiny.

Mr Daydream and Little Miss Tiny climbed onto its back and off they flew to the North.

North all the way to the North Pole.

"Look, there's a house with an upside down roof," said Little Miss Tiny as they flew on.

"Where are we?" she asked.

"We are flying over Muddleland," said Mr Daydream. "Would you like to have a look?"

"Yes please," said Little Miss Tiny.

In Muddleland everything is in a muddle and Christmas time is no exception.

In Muddleland they don't decorate their Christmas trees, they decorate their furniture.

In Muddleland they don't have Christmas lunch, they have Christmas breakfast.

And in Muddleland they don't hang Christmas stockings, they hang gloves above their fireplaces!

And then they were off again, and before long they found themselves flying over Cleverland.

Now as you can well imagine everyone in Cleverland is clever.

Even the sheep are clever.

So clever, in fact, that they celebrate Christmas.

Little Miss Tiny and Mr Daydream stopped off at many places on their way to the North Pole.

In Loudland, they heard the loudest carol singers in the world.

They were much too loud for Little Miss Tiny.

And they flew to Nonsenseland, where the snow is yellow!

"Just one more stop before we get to the North Pole," announced Mr Daydream, finally.

"Where is that?" asked Little Miss Tiny.

"Coldland!"

And it was. Cold, that is. Very, very, very cold.

And in Coldland they had tea with Mr Sneeze.

ATISHOO!!! sneezed Mr Sneeze.

ATISHOO! sneezed Little Miss Tiny.

"Oh dear," said Mr Daydream. "I think you might have caught a cold."

At last they reached the North Pole. Little Miss Tiny couldn't wait to meet Father Christmas. But where was he?

They landed beside a large chimney stack standing all on its own.

"How odd," said Little Miss Tiny.

Suddenly there was a rumbling sound and two big, black boots appeared in the fireplace.

"I think I need to lose a bit of weight," echoed a voice from the chimney. It was Father Christmas doing chimney practice with Mr Christmas!

And with a **POP** Father Christmas squeezed out of the chimney, covered in soot.

"Hello, there," he boomed to Little Miss Tiny. "How about a big tour for a little person? I've got to clean myself up, but Mr Christmas will show you round."

"Yes please," said Little Miss Tiny.

ATISHOO! she sneezed.

"Bless you," said Mr Christmas and Father Christmas together.

Mr Christmas led Little Miss Tiny into a large log cabin where she met the elves who were making all the toys.

ATISHOO! sneezed Little Miss Tiny.

"Bless you, bless you, bless you," chorused the elves.

Then Mr Christmas took Little Miss Tiny to feed Father Christmas' reindeer.

"Rudolf has a cold just like your one," said Mr Christmas.

ATISHOO! sneezed Rudolf.

"Bless you," said Little Miss Tiny.

And best of all they saw where all the presents were stored.

"And this one," said Mr Christmas, picking up a very tiny parcel, "is yours."

Little Miss Tiny's face lit up with excitement.

"It may be small," said Mr Christmas. "But Father Christmas won't forget to deliver it tonight."

And just then Father Christmas popped his head around the corner. He had dusted off his suit and it was bright red again. He was ready for his busy night.

Little Miss Tiny let out a small yawn. It was getting very late for a little person.

So Little Miss Tiny and Mr Daydream said goodbye to Father Christmas, Mr Christmas, the reindeer and the elves and climbed back on the enormous yellow bird. Little Miss Tiny could hardly keep her eyes open as they flew all the way home.

On Christmas morning, Little Miss Tiny woke to find herself sitting in her armchair, in her mousehole, in the skirting board, in the dining room, in Home Farm.

There, next to her tiny pinecone tree, was a parcel. Father Christmas had been!

"Gosh," she said to herself. "Did that Christmas holiday really happen?

Maybe it was just a dream?"

But then …

ATISHOO! she sneezed.